BRITAIN to colour

Book 1

1. Houses of Parliament, London
2. Urquart Castle, Loch Ness
3. Little Moreton Hall, Congleton
4. Crail Harbour, Fife
5. Caernarvon Castle, Gwynedd
6. Lanhydrock House Church, Cornwall
7. Cley Windmill, Norfolk
8. Kinloch Sperve, Mull

Book 2

A. Edinburgh Castle, Edinburgh
B. Scotney Old Castle, Kent
C. Eilean Donan Castle, West Highlands
D. Ribblehead Viaduct, Yorkshire
E. Stonehenge, Wiltshire
F. A Croft on Orkney
G. Cenarth Falls, Dyfed
H. Canal in Warwickshire

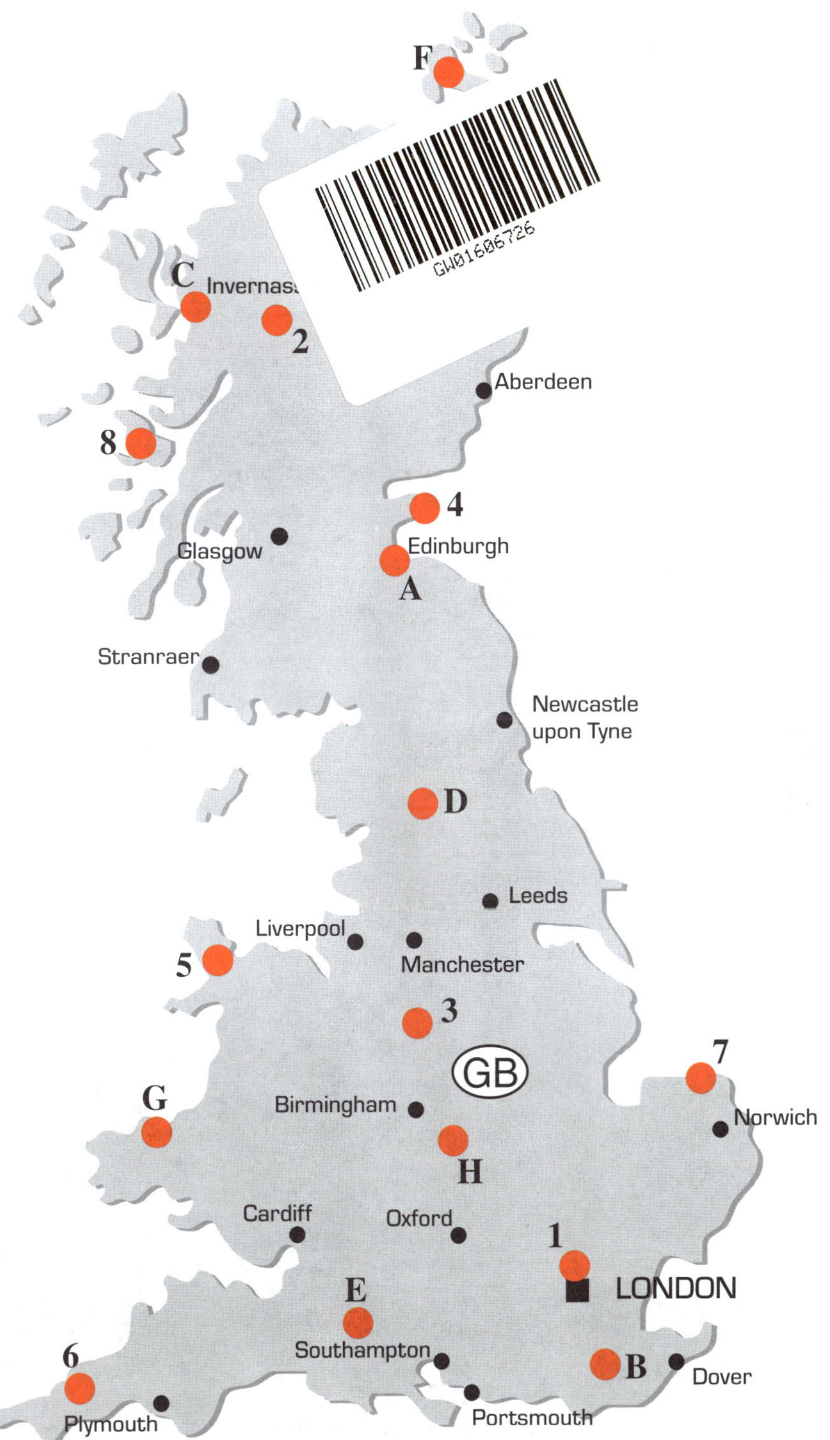

© Published by W. F. Graham (Northampton) Ltd, NN3 6RT
Illustrated by Jackie Brock, Thurso, Scotland
Further titles available:
Nature to Colour (4 titles) & Animals to Colour (4 titles)

Urquart Castle, Loch Ness

Little Moreton Hall, Congleton

Crail Harbour, Fife

Caernarvon Castle, Gwynedd

Lanhydrock House Church, Cornwall